W9-BUH-200

I MUST HAVE BOBO!

EILEEN ROSENTHAL

ILLUSTRATED BY MARC ROSENTHAL

ATHENEUM BOOKS FOR YOUNG READERS
NEW YORK   LONDON   TORONTO   SYDNEY

TO COFFEE DATES AND THAT CRAZY EARL

© 2011 BY EILEEN ROSENTHAL • ILLUSTRATIONS COPYRIGHT © 2011 BY MARC ROSENTHAL • ALL RIGHTS RESERVED, INCLUDING THE RIGHT OF REPRODUCTION IN WHOLE OR IN PART IN ANY FORM • SPECIAL DISCOUNTS FOR BULK PURCHASES, PLEASE CONTACT SIMON & SCHUSTER SPECIAL SALES AT 1-866-506-1949 OR BUSINESS@SIMONANDSCHUSTER.COM. • THE SIMON & SCHUSTER SPEAKERS BUREAU CAN BRING AUTHORS TO YOUR LIVE EVENT. FOR MORE INFORMATION OR TO BOOK AN EVENT CONTACT THE SIMON & SCHUSTER SPEAKERS BUREAU AT 1-866-248-3049 OR VISIT OUR WEBSITE AT WWW.SIMONSPEAKERS.COM. • BOOK DESIGN BY DAN POTASH • THE TEXT FOR THIS BOOK IS SET IN PP2DONART. • LIBRARY OF CONGRESS CATALOGING-IN-PUBLICATION DATA • ROSENTHAL, EILEEN. • I MUST HAVE BOBO// EILEEN ROSENTHAL ; ILLUSTRATED BY MARC ROSENTHAL. LOST AND FOUND POSSESSIONS—FICTION. 2. TOYS—FICTION. 3. CATS—FICTION.] I. ROSENTHAL, MARC, 1949- ILL. II. TITLE. • PZ7.R7194455IAE 2010 • [E]—DC22 2010004363

WHEN WILLY WOKE UP, THERE WAS TROUBLE.

OH NO! WHERE'S BOBO?

I *NEED* BOBO.

BOBO HELPS ME WITH EVERYTHING.

"BOBO, IS THAT A BITEY-BUG?"

BOBO'S NOT AFRAID TO GO DOWN THE SLIDE.

"HOLD TIGHT, BOBO!"

BOBO HOLDS MY HAND WHEN WE WALK
PAST THAT BIG DOG.

"DO YOU THINK HE SEES US?"

I MUST HAVE BOBO!

HEY! WHAT'S THAT?

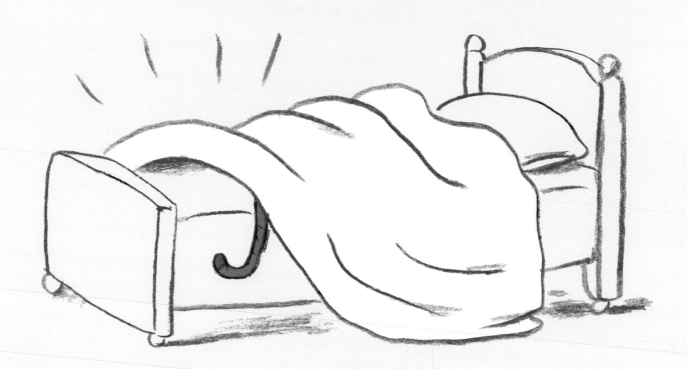

COME ON, BOBO. LET'S HAVE BREAKFAST.

BOBO THOUGHT WE WERE HAVING PANCAKES!

BOBO DOESN'T LIKE RAISINS IN HIS OATMEAL.

BOBO DOES LIKE COLORING.

YOUR HOUSE WILL BE BLUE, BOBO.

LET'S BUILD A FORT, AND EARL CAN'T COME IN.

LOOK AT ME, BOBO! BOBO?

WHERE IS THAT BOBO?

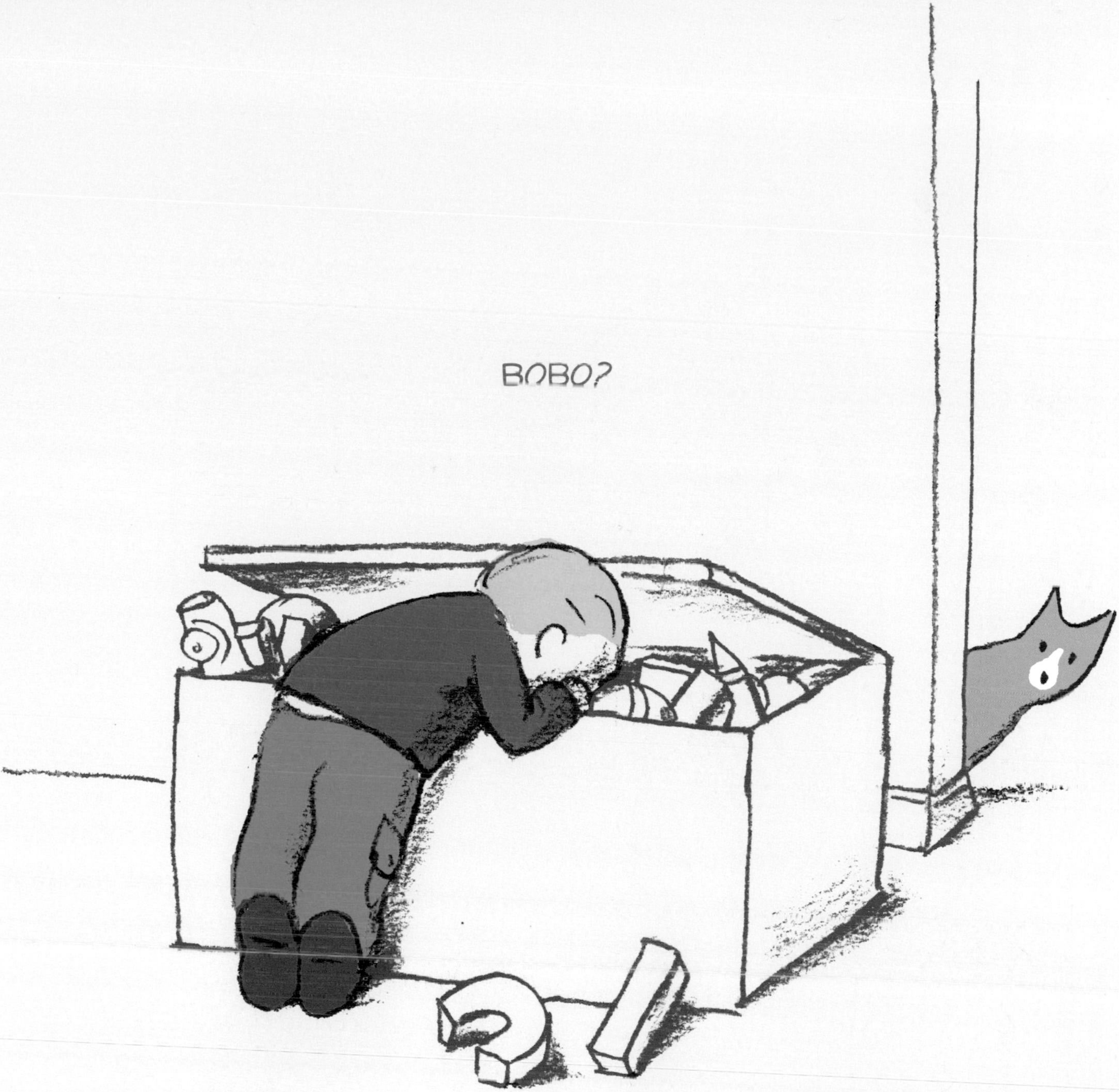

BOBO?

MAYBE HE WAS STOLEN BY PIRATES!

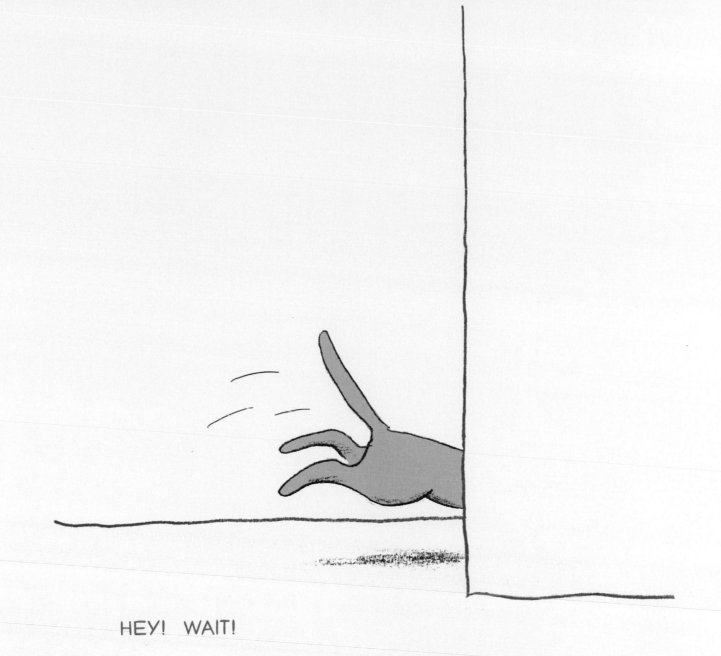

HEY! WAIT!

EARL, DO YOU HAVE
BOBO IN THERE?

BOBO!

EARL?

BOBO?

EARL?

BOBO! EARL!

HERE'S MY BOBO.